FOUR DECADES DEEP

AMAIRHA POKALA

To the person who recommended one of the best murder mysteries I've ever read to me, this story wouldn't have been completed without you.

Contents

Foreword   *vii*

Map of Basil Street   *ix*

1. Chapter 1   1

2. Chapter 2   6

3. Chapter 3   13

4. Chapter 4   18

5. Chapter 5   25

6. Chapter 6   33

7. Chapter 7   41

8. Chapter 8   51

9. Chapter 9   57

10. Chapter 10   65

11. Chapter 11   73

12. Chapter 12   77

Foreword

This story originally started as my attempt at trying something *way* out of my comfort zone. It quickly turned into a love letter to my friends, my neighbourhood, and my city.

I've drawn so much inspiration from the world around me that I started seeing the real people I know as characters and characters as real people - the lines eventually just started blurring.

The mystery/murder genre is still very new to me, but exploring it has been exhilarating. I truly hope you enjoy immersing yourself in the world of Basil Street and meeting its eccentric inhabitants.

Map Of Basil Street

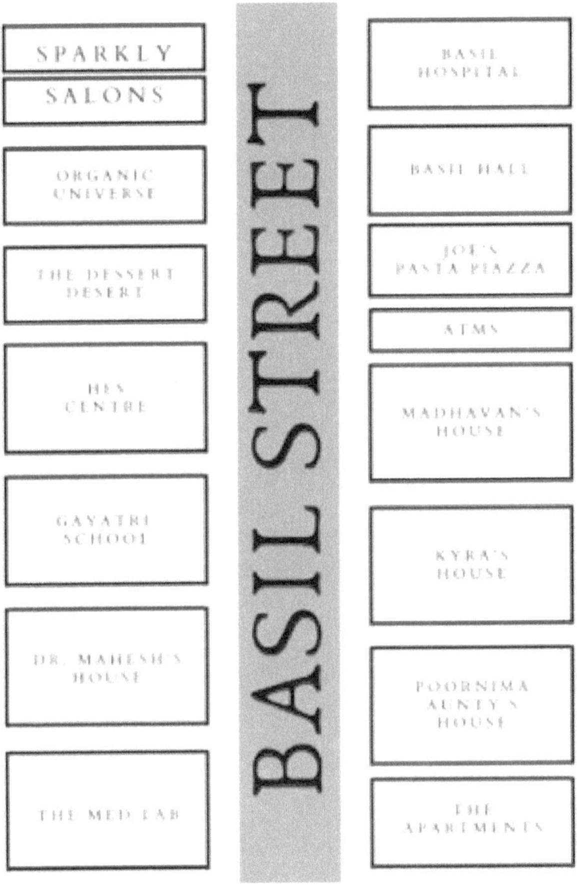

CHAPTER I

"Guys... I wish I didn't have to tell you this, but it's the harsh reality of our situation," Alana sighed. "We might have to shut down the agency soon."

"What!?" Ananya exclaimed.

Saanvi and Alana had co-led Volume 6 Private Eyes for the past 3 years. The detective agency had gained prestige after they successfully investigated the sudden melon shortage in Chennai's bazaars and caught the culprit red-handed. Ananya was a newer recruit. She had hopped on the bandwagon following the agency's success after the infamous contaminated groundwater case of 2021.

"I don't get it. We're the most prestigious and sought-after investigators in all of Chennai," she frowned. "We've made a name for ourselves, all while being sixteen-year-old girls."

"We *were* the most prestigious and sought-after investigators in all of Chennai. *Were*." Saanvi sighed. "Alana, could you give us the numbers?"

"There are no numbers," Alana checked her ledger. "Zero. Zilch. That's how many cases we've taken on this year. 2023 began 4, almost 5, months ago. Nobody's contacted us."

"I say it's because of misogyny! We have to overthrow the patriarchy!" Saanvi flashed them an evil grin, desperately trying to lighten the mood.

"Look, I know you're joking, but you could be right," Alana noted. "This *is* a male-dominated industry, after all. I don't blame people for not depending on teenage girls anymore."

"No, don't say that!" Saanvi patted her friend's hand. "I mean, come on. We solved those massive cases when we were *barely* fourteen. But, Ananya, that doesn't change the fact that we're shutting shop. Our last working day will be the first of May. Make sure to grab your stuff from HQ by then."

Volume 6's base of operations was Saanvi's guest room. The girls had made it their own by adding storage bins, bean bags, a small snack pantry, and hooking up their laptops to the pre-existing TV in the room to discuss cases.

"This can't be happening. Can't we just hire a social media marketing team to promote us? Run TV advertisements? Flyers, word of mouth, anything?" Ananya tried.

"We did think about it. We didn't want to give up on everything we've worked for. *Three years' worth* of blood, sweat, and tears," Saanvi replied. "But us staying open would just be futile."

"And, might I add, our social media presence isn't a problem at all. We have over 10 thousand supporters. Unfortunately, none of them are proving to be clients." Alana rose from her seat. "Saanvi and I have put a lot of thought into this decision. We'll meet here tomorrow at 1 p.m. for one last lunch at HQ. Bring boxes to pack your stuff in."

A sombre mood had set in across the room. Everyone mumbled their goodbyes, pushed their chairs in, and walked out of the soon-to-be-abandoned room.

• • •

The next day, all 4 girls gathered at Volume 6 HQ to sink their teeth into cheese sandwiches while segregating their belongings.

They leafed through old photo albums, fondly remembering the memories they had created together over the years.

"This one is from the day we dealt with the melon issue," Saanvi pointed to a picture of her, Alana, and Ananya each holding a gigantic crate of assorted melons. Muskmelons, watermelons, honeydew melons - they had it all.

"Oh, yeah. We didn't accept money back then, remember? This was our fee," Alana chuckled.

"This one's from the day I joined the team," Ananya held up a picture of herself clutching her shiny new Volume 6 Private Eyes ID card.

"Here's a picture from the day before that," Alana proudly displayed a Polaroid of the 2 original members standing in a pool of murky, runoff water.

"God, the groundwater incident," Saanvi laughed.

"This one was our first picture as a group." Alana showed everyone a picture of the 3 of them. She was cradling Saanvi's face, and Ananya was on her back. They gazed at the little piece of film fondly.

"Are... are you thinking what I'm thinking?" Alana said, a faint smile spreading across her face.

"Guys, guys, look," Saanvi interrupted, holding up her phone. A news website was open.

"70-year-old Chennai man brutally murdered in his Basil Street home, investigation ongoing," Ananya read the headline.

"*Woah,*" Alana gasped.

"Basil Street? That sounds familiar," Ananya pondered. "Oh, it's not too far from my house."

"Doesn't one of our classmates live there?" Saanvi asked.

They were interrupted by an urgent knock on the room's glass door.

"Kyra!" Saanvi snapped her fingers. "That's who lives on Basil Street!"

"And now she's at our door," Ananya peered at her.

Alana got up to open it. Kyra rushed inside, frazzled.

"I need your services," she panted.

CHAPTER II

Volume 6 had a corner of their headquarters slash meeting room reserved for talking to clients. The girls quickly led Kyra to an ottoman, where she plopped down. Saanvi and Ananya sat down across the table in front of her on 2 seats similar to hers, ready to question her. Alana prepared all the necessary paperwork that Kyra had to sign and pressed the *record* button on the old video camera they used to record their initial conversations with clients.

"It's standard procedure," Alana reassured her. "If we ever need any essential details while we try to solve this case, we refer to the recording. I need you to sign here for consent."

"Very old-fashioned. I like it!" Kyra grinned, scrawling her signature onto the sheet of paper Alana held. "I also like your fuzzy purple flamingo pen."

"Why, thank you! My colleagues will begin by asking you a few basic questions," Alana gave her a warm smile.

"What's your full name and age?" Saanvi asked, firmly but kindly.

"Kyra Reddy. I'm sixteen. Just like you guys."

"Where is your residence?" Ananya asked.

"33 Basil Street."

"How did you hear about us?" Ananya played with her pen.

"Oh, this is like one of those marketing questionnaires!" Kyra laughed. "You guys are my classmates, *and* you also happen to be the talk of the town. I thought you'd be the most reliable and safe option."

"We're adding that to our testimonials!" Alana laughed.

"You bet. This is the important question, Kyra. What brings you here today?" Saanvi looked her dead in the eye.

The girl fidgeted with her ring. "I'm sure you must have heard about the murder of Madhavan Srinivasan."

"He was your neighbour, wasn't he?"

"He *was*, and... I'd like you to conduct your own private investigation regarding who killed him."

"But the police force already has Detective Vardarajulu and his team investigating his murder. He's the city's top detective." Ananya cocked her head, confused.

"And we've never investigated a murder," Alana added. "Are we even eligible to do that?"

"Everyone's eligible to investigate a murder, and there's a first time for everything," Kyra pleaded. "I can explain why you need to do this for me. Charge me a steep fee, it doesn't matter."

"We're listening," Saanvi sank into a beanbag.

• • •

"Madhavan was our neighbour for a hundred years," Kyra began, a sandwich in hand.

"Isn't he only 70?" Alana asked, recalling the contents of the news article.

"Well, a hundred years in theory. His father, K.K. Srinivasan, purchased his property in 1923. The house was then passed down to Madhavan after he married Sunita aunty. He renovated it quite a bit - added this and that, tweaked the entrance and whatnot. My great-granddad Perugu Reddy also purchased our house in 1923, so our families have been friends for a century. My granddad grew up playing with him. I'm just telling you this to preface things - Madhavan and I were friends, I've spoken to him before, and he seems like a good person. Definitely not the type to have enemies. *Especially* enemies who are out for blood."

"So what you're saying is... nobody really had a motive to murder him?" Alana furrowed her eyebrows, deep in thought.

"Well, not that my family knows of. He could definitely be involved in private affairs. He just doesn't seem like the type. I'll walk you through a typical day for the man, alright? He wakes up at 7 a.m. and showers before (very loudly, might I add) doing his daily *puja*. He's a pious Brahmin. He eats breakfast at 8 and gets his grandkid ready for school. Oh, I forgot to mention that his son and daughter-in-law live with him. She's an architect and interior designer, and he works in IT abroad. They have one daughter. He's a retired college professor, so he spends the rest of the day watching television, playing cards, reading religious books, taking naps, and occasionally going on walks in his short shorts."

Saanvi chuckled. "Short shorts."

"Kyra, you seem to be really adamant about us investigating his murder. Why? Don't you have faith in the police?" Ananya asked, filled with curiosity.

"I don't."

Silence filled the room.

"Hear me out on this one. After Madhavan's murder, we were brought to his house by the police for questioning. They said it was standard procedure, just like this," Kyra gestured to the table and camera. "We obliged. I didn't appreciate being woken up at

6:30 a.m., though."

"One sec. Before we continue, Kyra, where was Madhavan's body found?" Saanvi piped up.

"Sunita aunty said she found him bleeding out in the kitchen because she usually wakes up early to cook breakfast."

"But you said he usually wakes up at 7 a.m.!" Alana snapped her fingers, quickly catching on. "Why was he up early?"

"Maybe he tried to fight off his murderer," Saanvi suggested.

"Maybe the killer dragged him to the kitchen to get a knife?" Ananya added. "Just reaching here."

"Wouldn't the killer have been armed already, though?" Kyra asked. "Saves a lot of time."

"The police should release a statement on his autopsy tonight," Saanvi noted. "We can think about the weapon then."

"Perfect! Kyra, do go on," Alana gestured to her.

"Right, where was I? We entered Madhavan's house at around 6:35. The police asked us basic stuff. We were sleeping, of course. We had surveillance footage from outside our gate as alibis. Just as my family and I were about to go back to our house next door, I noticed something. Sunita aunty was bawling her eyes out, but she stopped for a minute to slip an envelope to Detective Vardarajulu. The team cleared out of his house after gathering evidence by 7. I don't trust the police's investigation one bit."

"So you're suggesting..." Saanvi began.

"...that Sunita aunty bribed the detective into leaving early, possibly so he couldn't find any majorly incriminating evidence?" Ananya finished.

"I'm not suggesting anything, but... well, yes."

"Guys, it makes sense. Detective Vardarajulu joined the police force around the same time we started Volume 6, and he's already on top. How did he manage to gain his position and fame in under 3 years?" Alana gasped. "Kyra, you might be onto something."
"I think we might have to run 2 investigations at once," Ananya smirked.

"So... you'll look into his murder?" Kyra asked, her expression brimming with hope. "He was incredible. He deserves justice."

"That goes without saying!" Saanvi exclaimed. "This is the exact kind of publicity our agency needs. If we make a breakthrough and find the murderer, we won't have to close it! And, Kyra..." she exchanged a look with Alana, who nodded. "We won't charge you for our services if you join the team."

Kyra's face lit up.

"Oh my hair! YES! I would love to work for you guys!" she screamed, jumping.

"Work *with* us," Alana corrected with a smile. "We would love to have you, and you could provide some valuable insights on the case because of how well you knew Madhavan."

"It's settled, then," Ananya beamed from ear to ear for the first time that day.

CHAPTER III

They spent the rest of the day lounging at Volume 6 HQ until Saanvi bolted upright from her position on the rug.

"The police report is out!" she exclaimed. "Kyra, I've added you to our group chat. You'll find the link there."
"Oh, sweet, thanks!"

The girls rushed to open the link Saanvi had sent them. The room was filled with silence for a minute.

"What?" Alana spluttered. "Strangulation? But he was bleeding out!"

"If he was killed by strangulation, why did they find-" Ananya began.

"The entire blade of a kitchen knife inside his ribcage," Kyra whistled. "That's insane."

"This whole murder seems really poorly orchestrated," Saanvi noted. "The possibility of a struggle that led to Madhavan and his killer getting to the kitchen somehow? That's amateur work."

"Yeah, a hack job? This has to have been executed by a first-timer," Alana agreed. "On top of that, there's a chance that the knife didn't kill him so he needed to be strangled."

"Did Sunita aunty report any disturbances or noises?" Saanvi asked.

"No, she didn't. Everyone was positive that his murder was swift and silent," Kyra replied. "This report also mentions something about a break-in?"

"No, more like the lack thereof. There were few to no signs of a break-in. Whoever did this did a great job of covering up their tracks, but a hasty job of the actual murder." Ananya pressed her fingers to her temple.

"The police are also unable to find the handle of the knife that was used to kill Madhavan. It's missing from the crime scene," Alana pointed out. "But the blade gave away that the knife was from Hari's Household Appliances."

"I think we should head to Madhavan's place to talk to his family," Saanvi suggested. "It's only 6 p.m., and getting more perspectives on this situation will only do us good."

"Do you think we should confront Sunita aunty about the... you know?" Ananya asked. "I think we should save that titbit for a rainy day," Kyra proposed. "It could help us."

"Let's go, then," Alana threw the door open.

• • •

But first, tea.

There was a little tea shop near Madhavan's house. The girls gathered round a tiny table sipping steaming hot cups of milky, sweet tea.

The owner of the tea shop was seated on a little stool, staring at his phone.

"Oh, that uncle's so engrossed in whatever he's watching," Saanvi noticed.

"Uncle, which serial is that?" Kyra asked, suppressing a giggle. "I'm a bit of a Sun TV enthusiast myself."

"This isn't a serial, it's the news. This one guy who lives down the street was murdered today."

The owner of the shop pointed in the direction of Madhavan's house. "Detective Vardarajulu is talking to a news channel as we speak."

"Oh," Ananya set her cup down.

"*Oh*. Guys, we have to go!" Alana threw a hundred-rupee bill on the table as the group sprinted down the street.

They jogged up to an area sectioned off by caution tape.

"This wasn't here in the morning," Kyra noted. "Ugh. I need to get past this tape to get into my house!"

"Stop right there, trespassers!"

An old man appeared in front of them out of seemingly nowhere.

"Um, we're investigators," said Alana.

"No, you're not. You're children without any sort of authorisation to be here. Shouldn't you be filming dance videos or whatever kids do? This is a *crime scene, my* crime scene, Salt and Pepper Shekhar's crime scene!"

"Salt and pepper shake... oh." Ananya cackled. "Yeah, I see it. You should invest in some hair dye."

"Ananya, stop wasting time by trying to reason with the ageist comedic relief character. Mr. Salt and Pepper, we don't have a warrant, but we're reputed investigators. We just want to-" Saanvi began.

"*Investigators?* You children have watched way too much *Inspector Gadget.* I'm a forensics expert. I studied hard to get where I am today. You, on the other hand..." Shekhar spat on the road a bit too close to Kyra's feet. She leapt out of the way with a yelp. "Put the Nancy Drew books down and go to school. Study. Get married. Have babies. Look after them. Take my advice, and one day, when you're old and grey like me, you'll say *God, that Shekhar was a wise fellow who had my best interests in mind when he told me to* get out right now."

"Sir, you can literally Google us," Alana sighed. "Guys, this is pointless. Let's get out of here."
"Volume 6 Private Eyes," they heard from behind them.

They spun around, only to be met by the tall stature of none other than Detective Vardarajulu.

CHAPTER IV

The girls had never walked away from an experience with Detective Vardarajulu with a smile on their faces.

Of course, they were pretty much adored by the rest of the city. They received encouraging letters on a daily basis.

And this warmed their hearts, of course, but deep down, they yearned for Detective Vardarajulu's validation.

"He's just an old guy. I don't know why he's got us in a chokehold." Alana sighed.

"I think it's not exactly *him* - more so the fact that he keeps challenging us just because we're 'little girls' and we keep trying to prove him wrong, and we excel each time, and he still sticks his nose up and gives us the cold shoulder," Saanvi shrugged.

"Guys, he's trying to demotivate us. He's literally jealous, insecure, and worried we'll steal his job," Ananya banged the table. "It's obvious."

"I don't know about you guys, but I'm not too keen on working with the police," Saanvi retorted. "Stealing his job is definitely not one of my priorities."

"True that. I hate the... the system," Alana declared. "The system, yes. It's all messed up."

Detective Vardarajulu was not a homie.

• • •

"What are you little ladies doing here? Shouldn't you be at school?" Detective Vardarajulu raised an eyebrow.

"Mr. Detective, sir! That's exactly what I was saying!" Shekhar added.

"Detective, it's 6:30 p.m. on a Saturday," Alana responded, as professionally as she could. "Smack dab in the middle of our summer holidays."

"How was I to know that?" Vardarajulu snapped. "I don't operate on the schedule of a sixteen-year-old."

"The Botox gave that away," Ananya murmured.

"If you insist on knowing why we're here, Madhavan uncle was my neighbour and a close family friend. I just wanted to be in the know about what's going on," Kyra addressed the detective.

"Oh, you've acquired a fourth crony somehow! How much are they paying you to hang out with them?" Vardarajulu snickered.

"It was my choice to *work* with them, actually," Kyra retorted.

"Kyra?" they heard someone call out from behind.

"Poornima Aunty!" Kyra craned her neck to look at the source of the voice.

Poornima aunty was an old lady clad in a *kurta* and track pants - an odd combination of clothing, but nothing too out of the ordinary on Basil Street. She was jogging towards them.

"Detective, please leave these girls alone. They're just visiting me." Poornima gestured towards the bungalow that stood just a few metres down the road.

"Are you sure?" he replied, ever the sceptic.

"Positive. Hurry along, now."

The girls rushed past her gate and into her living room.

• • •

"Tea? Coffee? Juice? Soda? Chips? Biscuits? Chocolate? Sandwiches? Curd rice? Fruit salad?" Poonam offered.

"Aunty, I didn't know this was a restaurant," Kyra grinned.

"Oh, darlings, I just want to make sure you aren't hungry," Poornima blushed.

"Don't worry, aunty. We just drank some tea before... well..." Ananya exchanged quick glances with her friends.

"Before Detective Vardarajulu," Saanvi finished her sentence.

"He's such a menace. I wish he would focus on investigating Madhavan's murder and leave the rest of us alone," Poornima said, exasperated. "He's been bugging us since this afternoon."

She got up to slice some banana bread, bringing back a tray loaded with it.

"Yeah, I saw him pull up on my way out," Kyra confirmed. "That was in the afternoon. He's been here for ages."

"Anyhow, may I ask what you girls were doing at the crime scene?" Poornima said, setting the tray down.

Ananya picked up a piece. "Have you heard of an investigation agency called Volume 6 Private Eyes?"

"Oh, Kyra's mentioned it before. Some of her classmates run it, I believe," Poornima replied.

"We do!" Alana nodded. "Good to see you've been spreading the word, Kyra."

The latter beamed at her.

"Oh, my! I can't believe I'm in the presence of such talented young minds. Our groundwater isn't contaminated anymore because of you, little geniuses," Poornima exclaimed. "I'm assuming you're here to solve the case of Madhavan's murder?"

"Spot on," Saanvi confirmed.

"I'm afraid I don't have any good leads or anything. I was sound asleep until the police force woke us up for interrogation," Poornima recalled.

"Mm, so you didn't hear any sounds of distress?" Ananya asked.

"No, dear. Plus, I live pretty far away," she responded.

"Ah, no worries," Kyra munched on her bread. "We'll have to question a few more people on Basil Street before we approach the Srinivasans."

"Do you have anything that could aid us, aunty?" Alana inquired.

"Um, I have the street directory, if that helps," Poornima got up to retrieve a dusty book from the television cabinet, handing it to her.

"Oh, wow. I forgot these directories existed," Kyra inspected them.

"Thank you so much! This is perfect," Ananya stood up. "We won't impose further. We have loads to discuss. Thank you for the bread, aunty!"

"Oh, bye, girls! Feel free to stop by any time," Poornima said as she saw them out.

The girls jogged to Kyra's house, sprawled on her bed, and flipped the book open.

"This has everyone's contact information, details... and even where they work!" Alana noted.

"Oh, it even has a little baby picture of me! This book is *old* old." Kyra pointed to a picture on a page that had information on the residents of her house.

"And there's a map of Basil Street," Saanvi flipped to the first page.

"I know a doctor who lives next to The Med Lab," Kyra piped up. "Dr. Mahesh. He practices at Basil Hospital."

"What time does he leave the hospital?" Saanvi checked the time on her phone. "It's 7:15 now."

"Oops, we missed him. He leaves at 5:30 on weekends," Kyra sighed. "There's always tomorrow. He goes in at 2 PM on Sundays."

"Tomorrow it is. Maybe we could eat lunch at Joe's Pasta Piazza and question the owner. Two birds with one stone," Alana suggested.

"Oh, perfect. See you tomorrow, then!" Ananya nodded.

CHAPTER V

"Table for 4?" asked the host at Joe's Pasta Piazza. The restaurant was small, almost hole-in-the-wall. There were just 3 little tables in the quaint eatery.

"Yes. Are you the owner?" asked Alana.
"Yup. Nice to meet you, I'm Joe."

"Um, can we get the focaccia to begin?" Kyra asked. Joe nodded and disappeared into the kitchen, emerging with a bottle of water and 4 glasses.

"Okay, Mr. Joe," Ananya took a sip. "Is it okay if we interrogate you?"

"Uhm, is this for a school project?" Joe dragged a stool over to their table and plopped down on it. "I guess you could."

"Not exactly a project, per se. Have you heard of Volume 6 Private Eyes?" Saanvi reached into her pocket and dug around for a business card, sliding it across the table. Joe picked it up and examined it.

"Oh, a youth-led detective agency! Is that you guys?"

Alana nodded.

A light bulb seemed to go off in Joe's head. He looked pretty crestfallen.

"*Ahh*, this is about the Madhavan Srinivasan incident, right?"

"That's correct," Kyra bobbed her head in agreement.

"Well, let me go put your bread in the oven. I'll try my best to answer your questions once it's ready."

Joe sprang up and walked inside.

Ten minutes later, he was back, accompanied by a steaming plate of sliced focaccia that he set down on the table.

"So..." he began.

"Give us some background information about yourself, please," Alana pulled her phone out and began recording the conversation.

"My name is Joe Rigatoni. I'm 54, and I live right above Joe's Pasta Piazza, the restaurant I run. Fun fact, this is Basil Street's best- and only- Italian restaurant. I *love* the wordplay in the name, but you know what really upsets me sometimes? People often mistake the word 'piazza' for 'pizza.' 'Piazza' means 'public square' in Italian, and 'pizza' is a type of flatbread. How could you possibly mix them up? But anyways, I digress. I have a degree in culinary arts. I spent thirty years as the executive chef of the Dolomites' finest restaurant, and yes, as beautiful as Northeastern Italy was, I missed Basil Street."

"All roads lead here, right?" Kyra grinned.

"Exactly. This was home - no, it *is* home. So I saved up enough dough to move back to Chennai and live a comfortable life, but I missed cooking for people. The broker who found my apartment for me said the owner was also offering the commercial space below, so I bought the house and this restaurant and started Joe's last year. I've been living a quiet life here ever since. Nothing really eventful, until..."

"Until Madhavan's death," Ananya finished his sentence.
"It's really shaken up the neighbourhood. Everyone's afraid, and rightly so," Joe frowned.
"I understand. I live about a hundred metres away, and people on my side of the neighbourhood are frightened and concerned," said Kyra.

"Yeah. I come in at 11 a.m. because doors open at 11:30, so I usually get up pretty late. But this morning, I heard commotion and sirens, so I decided to investigate. I peered out of my window and saw Madhavan's body being carried away."

He inhaled.

"I'm so sorry, Mr. Joe," Alana patted his shoulder. "We're here to bring Madhavan justice by finding out who killed him and making sure they get what they deserve."

"He was a frequent customer. Loved my macaroni and cheese, and always got a mojito to go with it. He'd often buy a pizza for his wife to surprise her. The man loved Sunita dearly, and he always told me stories about their travels back in the '70s."

The girls exchanged glances. A few smudges of butter were the only remnants of the bread that were once on the platter before them.

"Thank you so much for your time, Mr. Joe," Saanvi smiled. "We'll be back, hopefully with good news."

The girls paid for their food, and Joe waved at them as they left the little eatery.

Back at Kyra's house, the girls collapsed on a sofa the minute they walked in.

"Well, now I'm confused," Ananya shrugged. "And we got so engrossed in what Joe had to say that we didn't even order our main course."

Saanvi laughed, but her expression turned sombre quickly. "Yeah. Madhavan really loved his wife, and he made sure to show it. Why would she orchestrate his murder?"

"Well, we don't know if she did it for sure," said Kyra. "We don't know the contents of the envelope she gave Vardarajulu. We just assumed it had money in it."

"What else could it have been? A love letter?" Alana smirked. Then she frowned. "I swear to God, if it was a love letter-"

"Alana!" Ananya playfully slapped her hand. "Well, the first thing we can do is gather as much information on him as possible. It seems like everyone in this neighbourhood has a Madhavan story."

"Oh, don't tell me we need to question all of them," Saanvi sighed. "I'm hungry."

"Me too," Kyra pouted.

"We can head to..." Alana glanced at the map. "The Desert Desert, grab something to eat, find an interview candidate, and then split up. We need to speak with Dr. Mahesh today as well."

The girls nodded and dashed out of the door, back onto Basil Street.

• • •

The Dessert Desert's interiors were just as uncanny as the cafe's name - and true to it. The walls were painted a sandy shade of yellow, and paper lanterns crafted to look like the sun had been hung across the ceiling. There were giant clay cacti in terracotta pots placed in every corner, and smaller real flowering cacti on every table. The chairs and tables looked like they were carved out of granite.

"How... creative," Alana noted. "And not kitschy in the least."

"Butter yellow walls aren't known for their subtlety," Ananya observed.

"It's so *camp*, I love it!" Kyra exclaimed, inhaling the sweet scent wafting towards them from the kitchen. "And it's pretty tastefully decorated for its size. I can't believe I've never been here before in all the years I've lived on Basil Street."

"Tasteful is... an adjective," Saanvi shrugged.

"I still don't get what camp means," said Ananya.

"Oh, you wouldn't," Kyra beamed.

The girls walked up to the display case, where a massive array of treats had been arranged in neat rows.

"Can we get one Mirage Mousse, 2 Cactus Cream Buns, and one Ghee Cake, please?" Saanvi smiled at the cashier.

"Ma'am, we don't sell ghee cake here," replied the cashier, "as you can see."

She turned red. "I'll just get the Camel Caramel Custard."

"Your total will be 6 hundred and sixty rupees."

The girls grabbed their desserts. "Is the owner of this cafe here today?"

"She's over at Organic Universe buying some brown sugar. She should be back soon."

They plopped their rear ends down on painfully uncomfortable, hard chairs.

"I have to say, this is pretty good," Saanvi swallowed a spoonful of custard.

"Is it as good as ghee cake, though?" Alana teased.

She shook her head. "Nah."

Just then, a tall lady carrying a jute bag walked inside the cafe.

Kyra tensed, almost dropping her dessert.

"Hi, dear! What a pleasant surprise!" exclaimed the woman.

"Meera aunty," Kyra smiled politely. The girls could sense that she was putting up a calm and collected front, but she was tense on the inside.

Just then, her face fell. "I'm - I'm so sorry for your loss. My family sends their condolences. If I'm not mistaken, they'll be visiting the house soon."

Meera was *tall*. The middle-aged woman was clad in a kurta, heaving what looked like a twenty-kilo bag of groceries and setting it down on a table that quivered under its weight. On hearing what Kyra had to say, she looked crestfallen.

"Uhm... yes," she began. "I'm sorry too - I mean, sorry for myself. No, I'm not sorry for myself. What am I saying? This is just an odd situation, I... I should just shut up."

She sank into a chair. "Nobody could have seen that coming, Kyra. Not me, not *amma*, nobody."

Kyra nodded. "I know, aunty. I can't imagine how you feel. Do you want to talk about it?"

Something clicked in Alana's and Saanvi's brains at the same time. They stared incredulously at each other.

"*What?*" Ananya whisper-yelled. "Guys, what's going on?"

Alana raised a hand to silence her. "Shh."

Meera buried her head in her hands. "I knew coming back to work this early was a mistake, but *amma* told me it would help me get my mind off of - of -"

She swallowed.

"*Appa's* murder."

CHAPTER VI

Meera and the girls had gathered around a large table. Alana and Kyra had taken turns consoling her, while Saanvi and Ananya listened intently as she vented - not out of sympathy, but because they knew every word she spewed could be a vital clue.

She didn't cry.

"Is that weird?" Saanvi would ask later on. "Let me rephrase. She didn't shed a single tear, however distressed she was. Is that suspicious?"

"I mean," Kyra began. "Maybe she processes grief differently."

"The majority of us were strangers to her anyway. Maybe that was a factor?" Saanvi suggested.

"Doubtful. She did pour her heart out to us without even learning our names," Alana shrugged.

After spending a solid hour with Meera, the girls diverged, agreeing to debrief on their encounter with her later that day. Alana and Kyra headed across the street to Basil Hospital to convene with Dr. Mahesh (Kyra had asked her uncle who frequented the clinic to let him know they'd be stopping by). Saanvi and Ananya decided speaking with the owner of Sparkly Salons was worth a shot.

"Excuse me," Kyra walked up to the receptionist. With a clipboard in hand, a stern expression on her face, and a pen tucked behind her ear, she was as intimidating as a middle-aged hospital receptionist could be.

"Erm, never mind," she took 2 steps back and nudged Alana. The latter sighed, approaching the scary lady.

"We have an appointment with Dr. Mahesh for..." she glanced at her phone's lock screen. "3 PM."

"A consultation?" asked the lady, looking them up and down.

"Not necessarily," Kyra trembled.

"It's sort of private," Alana added.

"I can see your slot on today's schedule, but I'm going to need the purpose of your visit, please," responded the receptionist.

"We're..." began Alana. "We're students-"

"Yes, we're students in charge of a youth magazine. And, as I'm sure you know, Dr. Mahesh is one of the most eminent, illustrious medical professionals on this street. It took us ages to secure this interview, and we want to make the most of it," Kyra smiled.

"Of course we do. We want to ask him important questions about the medical advancements of tomorrow," Alana smiled, catching her drift.

"Ah. In that case, please be seated. I'll inform the doctor of your arrival."

They covertly fist-bumped, shuffling to a corner.

The girls scrambled into the doctor's office-cum-consultation suite. After greetings and formalities had been taken care of, they were ready to ask Dr. Mahesh a few questions.

It turned out he had his own question to ask first.

"So, Kyra, has your uncle been taking his bowel incontinence medication? How was the gastroenterologist I referred him to? Dr. Kesavan, one of my friends from med school." Dr. Mahesh's face had taken on a wistful expression. "One of the finest of the batch of '75."

"I can't say I've inquired about his, um, bowel issues," Kyra began. "But I'm sure he's following his course. Strictly."

Alana stifled a giggle.

"Ah, you know, after a certain age, adult diapers are your best bet," the doctor nodded. "And trust me, I know. I've been trying to persuade him, but his ego's been getting in the way."

"Ah, I see."

"Yeah, take a look," Dr. Mahesh held up a pack of diapers with his face plastered on them. "My very own patented adult diapers that I made in collaboration with India's leading-"

"Lovely, lovely. I'll have to snag one of those before we leave." Alana forced a toothy grin before turning to exchange glances with Kyra.

Does this guy have no filter? Communicated Alana's glare.

Not that I know of, Kyra responded mentally.

"So, what brings you here today?" Dr. Mahesh asked. The girls breathed a silent sigh of relief. "Something to do with Madhavan, no? Such a gent. He had real class, I tell you. A man who knew how to make sound decisions. *He* knew when it was time to start using my diapers."

"Ew," Kyra muttered under her breath.

"Pardon?"

"Woah. I said *woah*."

"Yes, woah indeed. His death shook me to my core."
"He doesn't look very shaken to his core," Alana whispered.

"He was one of my most loyal patients to date, girls," Mahesh sniffed. "I've known him since we were in college. We grew apart later, but we've always been good friends."

"Was he healthy, per se?" inquired Kyra.

"Pretty much, dear. He did his last annual check-up right here and did his blood work at The Med Lab," replied Yeehaw. "Which, by the way, I am also affiliated with."
"I know. I use your name to get a discount there," Kyra began, cutting herself off. "Um, I digress."

"I see... anyway, the functioning of his organs was pretty standard. Nothing unusual. Oh, but there was something he never told his friends or his family."

"Oh?" said the girls in unison.

"I think now is as good a time as any to tell you, especially since you're investigating his murder," said Yeehaw, "Madhavan was..."

"Was..."

"A black belt in karate."

Alana nearly choked on air. Kyra had to cup a hand over her mouth to stop herself from guffawing at the prospect of the pudgy old man doing a roundhouse kick.

Then it dawned on them.

"Wait, what?" Alana spluttered.

"I was checking his reflexes and muscle functioning, and let's just say outward appearances can be deceiving."

"Tell me about it," Kyra murmured. "He looked like a bit of a teddy bear. Respectfully."

"I knew that *that* level of physical strength couldn't have been intrinsic, so I confronted him! Ha! I wrenched a secret out of Madhavan, one not even his wife knew!"

"But *how* could he have practised without being discovered?" Kyra pondered.

"And *why* would he want to keep his talent a secret?" Alana added.

"And *why* are we having a conversation this in-depth about karate?" quipped the doctor. "See, everyone has questions, and not all of them can be answered. He'd stay up late, practising in the wee hours of the night. I don't know why he wanted to hide his skills from the world. You'd need to look into his brain to know all about the man, but even peering into his mind wouldn't disclose all the information there is to know about him."

"Really?" asked Alana.

"Ah, this I know!" exclaimed Kyra. "Madhavan uncle was taciturn. He wasn't one to overshare. He mostly made minimal amounts of small talk. There aren't a lot of people who have truly bonded with him."

Dr. Mahesh bent his head in shame. "Alas, though I tried to make the man open up, I failed. After college ended, we all went our different ways until I moved to Basil Street and began practising here. The only thing I really found out after all those years was that he was a Mathematics professor and knew karate."

"God, who'd pick that career voluntarily?"

"I wouldn't, but I did sacrifice my social life to complete my MBBS, so maybe I'm not one to talk," Mahesh chuckled. "That was a joke. You guys can laugh at my expense."

Kyra and Alana let out throaty (and fake) laughs.

"Wait. I know he was a professor, but I never found out where he taught," Kyra piped up.

"Oh, the Indian Mathematics Institute. It's over an hour away from here. Poor guy, how did he handle the commute?"

The girls turned to each other and nodded.

"Well, Dr. Mahesh, you've given us plenty of information. Thank you for that," Kyra beamed.

"Yup, this conversation has been *unforgettable.* Thank you for your time." Alana pushed her chair out.

"Uh-uh-uh! You're forgetting this!"

Yeehaw grabbed a permanent marker, signed a pack of his adult diapers, and handed it to Kyra.

"For your uncle, from me!"

"Ah, thank you. I'll hand-deliver this to him," Kyra grimaced. "Bye, Dr. Mahesh!"

The girls skirted past the receptionist and out of the hospital. Ananya and Saanvi waved at them from across the street.

"ARE THOSE ADULT DIAPERS?" Saanvi yelled, a bit too loud for their comfort. She crossed the street, and Ananya followed suit.

"I think we should stop bringing these up," Alana snatched the pack from Kyra's hands, desperately trying to shove it in her tiny pocket.

CHAPTER VII

The girls sat down on a roadside bench near Joe's Pasta Piazza.

"How much does Madhavan's martial arts achievement really affect our case?" asked Ananya.
"A *lot*," Alana drummed her fingers on the table, deep in thought. "Ananya, think. If he had a black belt in karate, he would've been able to fight his attacker off in, like, a fraction of a second."

"Oh, okay, that makes a lot of sense."

"Before we hypothesise about that, what did the owner of Sparkly Salons say?" asked Kyra.

"Her name is Riya," began Saanvi. "Sparkly is divided into 2 separate salons - one for men and one for women. Madhavan got all his haircuts at the one for men. But, um..."

"He didn't have much hair to begin with," Kyra noted. "I respect that he wanted to look fresh, though."

"Exactly. Anyhow, she didn't provide us with a lot of useful information, but she did give us..." Saanvi reached into her pocket. "A buy-two-get-two-free voucher for pedicures!"

"Oh, how helpful," Alana noted dryly.

"I think we deserve them," Ananya shrugged.

"So all she said was that Madhavan cut his hair at Sparkly? Everyone on this street gets their hair cut at Sparkly. Not a massive deal, to be honest." Kyra frowned.

"Yeah, Sparkly was a bit of a bust. But anyway, Alana, what were you saying about Madhavan's karate?" asked Ananya.

"Yeah, so-"

Alana was interrupted by the blaring of sirens.

A Chennai City Police jeep pulled up to Joe's, and Detective Vardarajulu emerged from it. The detective, followed by a constable, barged into the restaurant.

"What's going on?" Kyra peered at the scene unfolding a few metres away from them.

The girls crept towards the eatery, carefully avoiding being noticed by Vardarajulu. They glanced inside.

"I'm - please, I'm a chef, not a murderer. I cook for this street, and the people here need me. Please. I'm sure I have an alibi," Joe begged.

"Mr. Rigatoni, your restaurant and flat are situated in a security camera blind spot. Please do not resist.

For the last time, you are being arrested for the murder of Madhavan Srinivasan. You have the right to remain silent, and anything you say can and will be used against you in a court of law. You have the right to an attorney."

Ananya gasped. Saanvi slapped a hand over her mouth.

Unfortunately, Vardarajulu had already spotted the girls standing outside the glass door.

"You 4," he hissed. "I hope you understand just how much power I have at my fingertips now. If you mess with me or my investigation, it's *over* for your little firm. I don't want to see you near Madhavan's house or meddling with the lives of this street's residents again. Do you hear me?"

• • •

Being an investigator comes with the knowledge of knowing when to back down. The girls, therefore, slipped away and headed back to Kyra's house.

But their investigation was *not* over.

"I think we should lie low for a little while," Alana sighed. "God, I hate that man so much."

"I've never been humiliated like that before," Kyra huffed.

"And Joe's been arrested for a crime we don't even think he committed," Saanvi added.

"And we're no closer to identifying the actual perpetrator," said Ananya. "Guys, things are not looking great for us right now."

"Look, we've put in too much effort to give up right now," Alana declared. "I know what we should do. We need to go over all the information we have."

And so they put their heads together.

"Alright, who are our suspects?" asked Alana. "From the top."
"Our first suspect is Madhavan's wife Sunita. Kyra said she saw her slipping a letter to Detective Vardarajulu..." began Saanvi.
"...which means he could've been an accomplice," said Kyra.

"Then there's Meera, Madhavan's daughter. There's no solid proof deflecting the needle of suspicion towards her *yet*, but her theatrics were a bit much. If they were theatrics," added Ananya.

"And finally, just because he doesn't have an alibi, Joe Rigatoni," Kyra frowned. "Poor Joe. I refuse to believe he had anything to do with Madhavan's murder."

"Is there any way we can clear his name? He could be a huge help in our investigation," pondered Alana.

"Actually, there is," Saanvi pointed to the map they had pinned to the bulletin board. "Joe mentioned he lives right above Pasta Piazza."

"Yes, he did say that."

"Alana, could you pull up Google Photos?"

Saanvi inspected the various photos of Joe's Pasta Piazza that customers had included in their Google reviews.

"This person took a picture of the restaurant's entrance," she pointed. "You can see Joe's window in it."

"Okay, but where is this going?" asked Ananya.

Saanvi was able to find a few photos of Basil Hall, the building neighbouring Joe's Pasta Piazza. She snapped her fingers. "See that branch over there?"

"Mhm."

"It's easily accessible from one of the first-floor windows in Basil Hall. Now check out that thicker branch. It extends right up to Joe's window."

"Saanvi, you're not suggesting..." Kyra's mouth dropped open.

"Look, the restaurant has been locked up. If we can break into Joe's house, we might be able to find something that'll act as an alibi," Saanvi shrugged.

"Just a suggestion, guys."

Kyra looked at Alana, who was deep in thought. "Alana, please don't tell me you're seriously considering climbing into Joe's house using a *branch*," she spluttered.

"I'm with Kyra on this. This is the most dangerous stunt you could ever pull," Ananya crossed her arms. "I'm putting my foot down, guys, and you *will* take me seriously."

"Kyra, Ananya, you guys don't have to join us. We'll need you to keep watch at Basil Hall," retorted Saanvi.

"You do know there are security cameras lining the street, don't you?" protested Kyra.

"Isn't Joe's restaurant in a blind spot? Who's to say Basil Hall isn't either?"

"Delusion," Kyra spat. "Delusion! Why would an events space frequented by people all the time be in a blind spot? I'm afraid you 2 are asking for trouble. There's got to be another way in."

Alana pulled her phone out and began typing furiously, as the others fell silent, watching her.

"Aren't you going to say anything?" asked Ananya.

Alana put her phone down. "One of my friends works at Basil Hall. She's an event coordinator and has access to the surveillance footage. I asked if she could disable the cameras temporarily, and she agreed."

"Woah," said Ananya.

"The other camera that we might be visible to is the one outside Organic Universe. That might be an issue. If it operates, there'll be a direct view of us breaking in."

"So you guys are definitely doing this," Kyra sighed, "and there's no way I can change your mind?"

Saanvi and Alana nodded.

"In that case..."

• • •

The girls found themselves on the road again, being led by Kyra towards Basil Hospital.

"Please don't make me go back to that doctor's office," Alana pleaded. "I'll do anything."
Kyra stopped in her tracks. "Will you promise not to climb into Joe's house via his window?"

Alana faltered. "Erm..."

"Relax. We're not going to the hospital."

"Where else, then?"

"We're going to Organic Universe," declared Kyra.

The girls exchanged confused glances.

"Look, I haven't really considered going vegan or keto recently... or at all, honestly," Saanvi chuckled. "And I *like* my food with added GMOs."

"And sulphates," added Ananya. "Oh, and don't forget the preservatives. We love those."

"How on Earth are you guys some of the most accomplished investigators I know despite always jumping to conclusions?" Kyra spluttered. "I'm not buying you guys organic food!"

"Baffles me too," Alana shrugged. "So why are you taking us there, then?"

Kyra stopped walking. She gestured to a bench on the sidewalk. The girls sat down.

"Do you guys know Oriental Express, that Chinese restaurant about 5 minutes from here?" she asked.
"I've heard of it, but never been," revealed Alana.

"I love a bit of literary wordplay!" Saanvi grinned.

"I really, really love the lemon chicken there," said Ananya solemnly.

Kyra laughed. "My family owns that restaurant, and Organic Universe supplies all our vegetables."

"I'll be expecting a discount the next time I visit," Ananya smirked.

"Sure. Anyways, we know the owners of that store. They've been our suppliers for more than a decade now, so I'd say we're close."

"Go on," said Alana.

Kyra inhaled. "Basically, Organic Universe has access to the controls of the security camera facing Basil Hall. That's the only camera that would capture you guys entering Joe's place."

Saanvi's face lit up. "Okay…"

"If we were able to explain our investigation to the owners, they might let us disable the camera for a *bit*. I'm talking no more than fifteen minutes."

"Kyra, that's perfect!" Alana cheered. "Does that mean you're fine with us breaking and entering?"

Kyra shuddered. "Oh, please don't put it like that, I pray. But yes, I suppose we should put our all into a high-stakes case like this."

"What she means is that *you*," Ananya pointed at Alana, "and Saanvi are putting your all into this."

"We'll keep watch from the room above Organic Universe," added Kyra. "Far, far away in a land without a single possibility that we might end up convicts."

"Pfft," said Saanvi.

Negotiations began shortly after with Mahendran and Kalpana, the kind couple that owned Organic Universe. After much convincing and debriefing about safety concerns (people the age of your parents *will* be people the age of your parents), they finally agreed to disable the cameras.

"For a good cause," sighed Mahendran.

"If we disable the cameras for more than 10 minutes, though, we'll have to answer to the neighbourhood organisation," Kalpana warned. "That could end badly for us. We'll still keep them off for fifteen minutes just for you."

"Building a good reputation among the neighbourhood watch helps, girls," chuckled Mahendran. "You never know. Organic Universe would make a great fro-"

"Off his meds again," mumbled Kalpana, grabbing her husband's wrist. "Anyways, when are you doing this?"

Alana and Saanvi exchanged a glance.

"Now, climbing those branches will be easier before the sun sets."

"Oh, *Govinda Swamy*," muttered Mahendran. "Kids these days..."

CHAPTER VIII

"Basil Hall was originally a residential house," explained Kyra. "The lady who lived there really, really, *really* loved shopping. She had it converted to a hall for people to sell their products. Designers, bakers, perfumers, you name it. The exhibitions she hosted were renowned far and wide."

"All you really need is passion for something, huh?" grinned Saanvi.

"Mm. She retired and moved to Australia, but the neighbourhood organisation still organises exhibitions and leases it out for private events. I celebrated my 3rd birthday here."

"Enough chit-chat, guys," Alana snorted. She flashed a thumbs-up at Ananya, who swiftly disabled the camera.

Alana and Saanvi rushed inside the building, zipping up the stairs until Kyra could see their faces through the first-floor window. She waved.

Wait a minute, how are they going to get that thing open? She pondered. The window swung open.

"How?" yelled Kyra.

"Hairpin," Saanvi shouted back.

Huh, seems an awful lot like something a lazy author would do to try and avoid a plot hole, thought Kyra. She shrugged, checking her watch. "Hurry!"

The pair hopped onto the branch one at a time, shuffling across. Saanvi used her hairpin to get Joe's window open, and they slipped inside.

Kyra spotted them rummaging through drawers and flipping through books.

"Couldn't stay away for long enough, hmm?"

Kyra turned to her left, gasping at a face with a devious smile plastered on it. She shrieked.

● ● ●

"You girls really thought you could make all that racket on the street," began Detective Vardarajulu. "Force an innocent couple to disable a security camera, the use of which was mandated by *law*, and most importantly..."

He inhaled with the force of a mighty hurricane.

"YOU WENT AS FAR AS BREAKING AND ENTERING," he yelled, moustache curling, spittle flying out of his mouth, "INTO THE HOUSE OF A CONVICT!"

Ananya cringed.

"You girls aren't leaving this station today, oh no, no, no," he fumed. "Thank goodness my good friend Shekhar was patrolling the streets. He's the only one who can deal with you brats!"

"Brats!" Shekhar spat. "You're no Hercule Poirot, you're a bunch of Poi-rats!"

Shekhar and Vardarajulu shared a hearty laugh. Kyra joined in weakly.

"What? It was a good joke."

Silence.

"You plebs, you wouldn't get it."

"It's really hard to laugh when you're being detained at a police station, Kyra," Alana mumbled under her breath.

And so they were. Complete with an exposed brick wall so rustic, it would've made a bachelor pad look modest in comparison, and the slogan 'TRUTH ALONE TRIUMPHS' emblazoned on the wall in all caps, the local police station was a short walk away from Basil Street. It was... unwelcoming, especially in comparison to Poornima aunty's cosy living room or Joe's quaint restaurant.

"Hold on a second, is Joe in here?" blurted Ananya.

Detective Vardarajulu roared, "I don't think you understand the weight of what you girls have just DONE!"

He slammed his hand down on the desk at which Chief Inspector Kumaran sat, munching on a *vada*. The pot-bellied old man nearly jumped out of his seat. He then went back to sipping a cup of tea, watching the scene intently.

"There's no way *this* is the plight of our system," Saanvi scratched her head in disbelief.

"Look, Detective," argued Alana, "we weren't trying to stir up any trouble by, as you put it, breaking and entering into Joe's house. You and I both know he's innocent. You're just too incompetent to actually put effort into this case and think sweeping it into the dustbin will sort everything out."

Vardarajulu's ears turned pink.

"I'm going to ignore you, little girl," he hissed. "What on Earth do you think you could have found there?"

"We all have names, Detective," Ananya snapped. "I don't think the words 'little girl' are mentioned even once in Alana's birth certificate."

"I feel like you kids don't know who you're dealing with," piped up Shekhar. "This is *the* Detective Vandukrishnan Vardarajulu. He could mess with your lives big-time, but he isn't because he knows you'll grow out of this little investigator phase someday and actually get your lives together. You get me, hmm? He's showing you sympathy. The least you could do is recognise that he solved a pressing case in just a few days and leave this department alone."

Inspector Kumaran spoke for the first time that evening. "Look, you've done some great work in the past, but we've nabbed the culprit now. You should let this go."

"Based on what evidence," began Kyra.

Shekhar's phone rang. At first, the girls thought he had opened Spotify by mistake because the most obnoxiously upbeat Kollywood song was penetrating their eardrums. But it was indeed a call. Someone really opened their contacts list and tapped Shekhar's name.

Deliberately.

Wild, I know.

He perked up as Inspector Kumaran continued to advise the girls. "If you're really committed to this whole quasi-career you have going on, maybe revisit it in a few years. You know, college will be an amazing opportunity for you to branch out and discover new hobbies. Shekhar, what's wrong? You look like you've seen a ghost."

Shekhar put his phone in his pocket, hands shaking. "D-Detective, Inspector... there's been another murder on Basil Street."

CHAPTER IX

"That means Joe's innocent!" Ananya exclaimed. The girls jumped off the bench they were seated on. "You were wrong!"

"Silly girls, it needn't have been the same person behind both the murders. It might have been an accomplice of Joe's." Vardarajulu chuckled.

Shekhar trembled. "Erm, Detective... whoever did it left a note."

He showed Vardarajulu a picture on his phone.

Ananya snatched the phone out of his hand deftly. Her eyes flitted across the screen. She gasped.

"I killed Madhavan, and now I've killed Mahesh," she read. "If you don't want the entire population of Basil Street to be wiped out, well... Detective Vardarajulu, you know what to do." Detective Vardarajulu paled. "It can't be. The culprit behind Madhavan's murder is sitting in a cell and being monitored by my team."

"You dense fool, the murderer is still out there!" Kyra cried. "Can you put your ego aside for 2 minutes and think about the people who live on Basil Street— including *me*? Our lives are at risk. The killer got Dr. Mahesh, and any of us could be next if we don't get him!"

Vardarajulu inhaled. "Have you girls found any leads?"

Alana grinned sheepishly. "Well, sort of. We were thinking of Mrs. Madhavan, but..."

"There's really no solid evidence," Shanaya finished.

"Are you insane? There's no way it could be her," Shekhar laughed out loud.

Vardarajulu nodded. "I've been friends with her - and Madhavan as well, formerly - and I'm convinced she'd never do it."

Ananya was startled. "You mean you *know* the couple? You've got access to so much more information than us, and you still falsely accused Joe!"

Varadarajulu sighed. "Look, I think we're better off conducting our own separate investigations."

"Are you saying what I think you are?" Kyra raised her eyebrows,
"As long as you don't interfere with my business, I'll leave you to yours. Just don't stick your noses into places they don't belong," Vardarajulu huffed, ambling out of the station followed by Shekhar.

The girls sped after them before Inspector Kumaran could finish his fourth *vada*.

• • •

"Okay, so now we-" began Alana.
"No, Alana!" snapped Ananya. "We've *just* gotten out of a police station. A police station," she repeated for emphasis. "We can't afford to do reckless things anymore. I'm beyond shocked Vardarajulu even let us go."

"It's partly my fault for giving them a plan," sighed Kyra.

"Well, Ananya, maybe you should've spoken up and been more firm with us about how you actually felt," huffed Shanaya. "There's no point in blaming us for something that's *over*."

Ananya opened her mouth to make a retort, but Alana stepped in front of her. "Guys, please. We really can't fight right now. We need to work on figuring this out. We didn't talk to all those people and do all that research for nothing."

The girls kept walking in silence as a squadron of police cars zipped past them, sirens blaring, towards Dr. Mahesh's residence. Heads lowered, they dragged themselves along the sidewalk. Eventually, Kyra spoke up.

"Uh, I think we passed my house already," Kyra looked to the left. "This is Poornima Aunty's place."

"Is she hosting a party or something?" Ananya pointed at the line of cars parked outside the compound.

"I'm actually not sure."

They walked up to the gate, peeking into one of the house's ground floor windows.

"I can't believe my eyes," laughed Ananya. "Guys, come look at this."

Poornima aunty, clad in a *sari* and apron, was directing what looked like a Pilates class in the living room from her stool in the kitchen. She waved a ladle around, pointing at random students while cooking.

"She's definitely a... multitasker," commented Shanaya.

"She's actually really skilled at yoga and Pilates. She started training decades ago, from what I've heard. I didn't know she took lessons, though," said Kyra.

"Do you think she'd mind if we stopped by?" asked Alana.

"Probably not, to be honest. It looks like class is ending."

The girls walked up to the front door, knocking on it. An elderly woman wearing a T-shirt and joggers opened it.

"Hi, we're friends of Poornima Aunty," Kyra waved.

"Oh, the young'uns!" exclaimed the lady. "Poornima, the detectives have come to see you!"

"We're actually private investigators," responded Alana, but before she could even close her mouth, the girls were swarmed by old ladies.

"Is it true that you little ladies met the Prime Minister?"

"Are you really investigating a murder?"

"I have 4 grandsons and they're equally intelligent and handsome," one of them grinned. "They're quadruplets!"

"Interesting," said Shanaya. She was silenced by a glance from Alana.

"Make way!"

Poornima aunty pushed her way through the crowd.

"Hi, girls. I'm so sorry about my students; please ignore their antics."

"We're not just any students, we're her childhood friends!" exclaimed one of the women. "Batch of 1975!"

"Oh, that's..." Alana forced a smile. "Absolutely lovely."

Poornima's brows furrowed. "Sweetheart, are you alright?"

She turned around. "Ladies, clear out. Our next class is *on the* day after *tomorrow* at 5."

"P.M. or A.M.?" someone called.

"A.M.!" someone else exclaimed, as the women filed out of the front door, lugging massive duffel bags along.

The girls spotted Kalpana from Organic Universe. She revealed that she had been a long-time student of Poornima aunty.

Alana, Shanaya, and Kyra plopped down on the living room sofa as Ananya followed her nose. It led her to the kitchen, where a pot of *biryani* was cooking on the stove.

Poornima laughed. "Can I offer you some *biryani*, girls?"

"Appreciate it, but I'm a vegetarian," Kyra smiled politely.

"Oh, darling, so am I. This is vegetarian *biryani*." Ananya's head snapped up in alarm. She sprinted away from the pot as everyone else burst into peals of laughter.

"Oh, you carnivore!" Shanaya spluttered.

"I'm glad you're feeling better now," grinned Poornima. "I just heard sirens a few minutes ago. Do your long faces have anything to do with that?"

"Aunty, Dr. Mahesh was murdered," Kyra choked out.

"Erm, I hope that news wasn't confidential," murmured Alana.

Poornima paled. "Wasn't the killer - that Joe guy - put behind bars today?"

"It isn't him, aunty. Tonight's murder was concrete proof of that. There's someone targeting Basil Street residents - someone on the loose." Shanaya's voice cracked.

"Oh."

Poornima's eyes welled up with tears. "Why are they targeting *innocents*?"

"Aunty, please don't cry!" exclaimed Alana. "We're on the case."

The silence that filled Poornima aunty's warmly lit living room was deafening.

CHAPTER X

Early the next day, the girls found themselves ascending the stairs behind Joe's Pasta Piazza and ringing his doorbell.

Just before that, they had stopped by Dr. Mahesh's house. They discovered from the staff there that just like with Madhavan, Mahesh had been killed by strangulation. That meant there was definitely some sort of correlation between the 2 events - nothing about this seemed coincidental.

Joe, with his dishevelled hair and dark circles, looked like he had just fought a dozen wars. His eyes lit up when he saw the girls.

"Joe!" they exclaimed. When they noticed his exhaustion and physical appearance, they grimaced.

"Girls, please come in. Yesterday was crazy."

He forced a weak smile, leading them to the dining table. "Have you eaten yet?"

They shook their heads, no.

In a few minutes, he set a platter piled high with toast onto the table. "Help yourselves, I'll fill you guys in."

. . .

"Being locked up in that cell..." he shuddered. "It was horrible. I'm a common man all alone in this city. I've got no family here, and no close friends either. I was interrogated for a good 2 hours, and I told them I was innocent. I told them Madhavan was a person I truly cared about. I told them exactly where I was the morning of Madhavan's murder. Nothing worked, girls. I almost gave up hope."

"Joe, we tried breaking into your house to see if we could find any evidence that could act as an alibi," Kyra confessed. "But that ended really badly for us because we ended up being detained at the police station."
"And Vardarajulu told us off, which was the worst part," Ananya huffed. "But somehow, he gave us permission to carry on our investigation."

Joe's mouth dropped open. "I think I need a minute to process that."

Alana laughed. "It's true. Shanaya and I climbed in using the branches of the tree outside Basil Hall."

Warmth slowly spread across Joe's face as the corners of his mouth turned upwards into a smile.

He doubled over, laughing until tears streamed down his cheeks.

"Oh, girls, I needed that," he panted.

"We're dead serious. We literally climbed in," chuckled Shanaya.

"I know!" he beamed. "But seriously, thank you so much. I really appreciate that you were willing to go through all that for me - and get caught in the process."

"You've been really kind to us, Joe. It's the least we could do," said Alana. "Well, we just wanted to check in. We need to go do some serious contemplation."

"What about?"

"Our very existence."

• • •

The girls decided the best thing they could do at that moment was head to Dr. Mahesh's house and see if there was anyone they could speak to. Fortunately, Alana had just received the glossy, professional-looking ID cards she had ordered for them.

"At least we can't get denied entrance to crime scenes now," she shrugged.

Dr Mahesh lived in a stark white bungalow that had been sealed off with yellow caution tape. Kyra shuddered at the flashbacks running through her mind to the scene she had witnessed 3 days prior.

There was a police officer at the scene. He let the girls through after they presented their IDs, informing them that Dr. Mahesh's wife wasn't receiving visitors but would probably make an exception for investigators.

"Excuse me?" Shanaya called, stepping into the house. "Volume 6 Private Eyes. We're investigators."

Mrs. Mahesh descended the stairs, her face tear-streaked. She swallowed, gesturing towards the living room. "Sit."

"Madam, we're really sorry about the loss you've suffered. We're working to get justice delivered to you and Mrs. Madhavan," said Kyra.

Mrs. Mahesh nodded. She clearly wasn't a lady of many words. Then again, she was grieving.

"Could you tell us about the murder? At what time did it take place?" asked Ananya.

"Around 10 minutes past 6 in the evening. Kitchen. His pulse had just stopped, and there were slashes on his body," she choked.

All 4 of the girls exchanged glances.

"Was there nobody else in the house? No signs of a break-in?"

"No. It was a Sunday, so the staff was on leave. I was upstairs getting ready. We were about to leave for dinner."

"May we inspect the kitchen?" requested Alana.

Mrs. Mahesh nodded. "The police stayed here till late last night, cleaning up the scene and whatnot, but you can still take a look."

The kitchen was spotless, with squeaky-clean tiled floors and glossy laminated wooden cupboards. Ananya bent over to admire the sparkling silverware set on a counter.

"Mahesh was a germaphobe," explained his wife.

"Makes sense. His consultation suite looked super clean as well," noted Kyra.

"We found him over there, right beside the fridge," said Mrs. Mahesh, gesturing to the massive refrigerator. It was *huge*, big enough to fit 2 adults inside.

"Interesting. Well, thank you for your time. We really hope we can solve this case as soon as possible," Alana nodded at the woman who escorted them to the door.

"That was a really big fridge," noted Shanaya. "But that visit didn't help us out much."

"Yeah, Mrs. Mahesh really wasn't in the mood to talk," agreed Ananya.

"Guys, you still haven't spoken to my family yet. They've known Madhavan for *years*!" exclaimed Kyra.

"She's got a point. How are they placed this evening?" asked Alana.

• • •

Later that day, the girls sat down at Kyra's dining table as her dad brought out a pitcher of juice and a tray of sandwiches.

"Girls, how can we help you?" asked their mom.

"Aunty, Kyra tells us you guys have known Madhavan and his family for decades now. Is there anything you think we might not know about him that we should?" Shanaya asked, filling a glass with juice.

"Well, did Kyra tell you that he was a Mathematics professor?" said Kyra's uncle.

"She told us all the basic stuff about him and his kids."

"Well, aside from that, he lived a quiet life, especially when he got older. I do recall him being quite rambunctious during his youth - as we all were, to be fair," laughed her grandpa.

"Oh, I remember you mentioning this when we were younger. Madhavan and his gang, the Magnificent Men," laughed Kyra's mom.

"What on Earth is that? A movie about aeroplanes?" chuckled Kyra.

"Well, at least you know where they got the inspiration for that name. No, Madhavan and 3 of his other friends formed a gang way back when they were in college. It consisted of Madhavan, Dr. Mahesh from down the road, Mahendran, the owner of Organic Universe, and Madhan, the principal of Gayatri School," explained her uncle.

"They formed it because all their names started with the letter M - a silly reason, I know, but back in the day, they hosted famous parties and caused quite a ruckus. That was why it surprised me so much when most of them did a full 180 and quietened down," laughed Kyra's grandpa.

The girls weren't laughing.

"I think we're just gonna go up to my room for a bit," said Kyra, as the 4 of them sprinted up the stairs, slamming the door to her room behind them.

"The knife in Dr. Mahesh's chest," said Alana, panting furiously.

"The fact that both the murders have targeted members of Madhavan's old college gang!" Shanaya put her hands in her hair. "Guys, guys, guys, I think we've cracked it."

"*Everything* has had a pattern. Madhavan was murdered at 6:10 a.m., and Mahesh at 6:10 p.m." Kyra added.

"Both the murders happened one day apart!" exclaimed Ananya.

Kyra checked the date on her phone. "Mahesh was killed yesterday, and Madhavan was killed 2 days ago. That means the next murder will be..."

"Tomorrow," said Alana firmly. "I know what we have to do."

CHAPTER XI

At five-thirty a.m. the next morning, the girls assembled at Kyra's. Dressed in black, they looked straight out of a spy movie.

"We're so Mission: Impossible coded!" squealed Ananya.

"More like Barbie: Spy Squad, if you ask me." snorted Alana.

"In proper crime thrillers, they call this a stakeout," stated Kyra matter-of-factly.

The plan of action was as follows: Kyra and Alana would head to Mahendran's house above Organic Universe, whereas Shanaya and Ananya would wait at Gayatri School, where Madhan's quarters were located. They had met with the 2 last night, explained everything that was happening, and made them swear to secrecy.

"Mmm, steakhouse," sighed Ananya. "I could eat."

If any of the girls found themselves in a physical altercation with the killer, they'd call for backup. They had conferred with Detective Vardarjulu and Shekhar to have 2 groups of officers at the ready - one hidden in Basil Hall, the other in Kyra's house.

"This is it. The culmination of our career. The riskiest thing we've ever tried to pull off," declared Ananya.

"Even riskier than when we climbed a tree," noted Shanaya. "I digress. We should head out."

"I'm just so confused. Why is the killer targeting a college friend group that disbanded over forty years ago?" Kyra cocked her head.

Alana frowned. "We'll know soon enough. This killer... he or she was able to defeat a seasoned karate expert. If you spot them, I want you to call for backup *immediately*. Don't try and fight them off. You don't want to end up like Madhavan and Mahesh."

"What if I do?" teased Shanaya.

"Very funny."

• • •

ALANA AND KYRA
Alana and Kyra got into position in Mahendran and Kalpana's living room. The clock ticked rhythmically in the kitchen. They took deep breaths, steadying themselves. It was almost 6.

SHANAYA AND ANANYA
Shanaya and Ananya squeezed into a small guest bathroom near Madhan's kitchen with the door

slightly ajar. Five minutes past 6. Any time now.

ALANA AND KYRA

6:06. The girls heard a creaking noise from the kitchen, as if a cupboard was being opened.
They looked at each other. Nobody had entered the house since they had. Had the killer arrived even earlier?

SHANAYA AND ANANYA

The other 2 had heard a similar noise from the kitchen, followed by a loud thud.
Hands trembling, they looked at each other for confirmation and called for backup.

ALANA AND KYRA

They called for backup, trying their best not to hyperventilate. They knew they were in the presence of a killer – it felt like the entire weight of their situation was dawning on them all at once.

SHANAYA AND ANANYA

It was all a blur as Ananya, Shanaya, and the police burst into the kitchen and switched on the lights, finding Madhan cornered by *her*.
"You!" they gasped.

ALANA AND KYRA

Alana and Kyra followed the police into the kitchen when they saw *her* with her hands stretched out.
Kyra screamed.

• • •

That was how they found themselves at the police station's interrogation room with Detective Vardarajulu, Kalpana, and Poornima aunty.

Poornima smirked. "How ingenious of you, little girls. You caught us in the act."

Kyra was sobbing. "I can't believe you'd do this. You killed Madhavan. He was an innocent man."

She pointed at Kalpana. "She tried killing your husband, and you *helped her* - and you almost got Madhavan!"

"You silly girl, I didn't kill Madhavan," snorted Poornima. "You wouldn't understand why we did all of this."

"Make us understand, then," snapped Alana, "if your motive was good enough to warrant 2 murders."

Poornima laughed maniacally.

CHAPTER XII

"Well, alright, then. But we'll have to rewind things to the late '70s - 1978, to be exact."

Kalpana and I were fresh out of high school and 3 years into college. At the time, I was seeing Madhavan. Oh, don't be so surprised, little girls. I was young once, and I had a life before I became the widower I am now.

You probably know this already - maybe that's how you pieced everything together, you *smarty pants* - but Madhavan, Mahesh, Mahendran, and Madhan had this little gang thing going on. Notorious for their bad behaviour - always driving around on their bikes, skipping classes, hosting parties, whatnot. I used to go out with them whenever I wasn't studying. I assumed everything they did was in good fun. That was until the Magnificent Maniacs killed my best friend.

Oh, just let me finish. They *did* kill her. One night, they pressured her into jumping off a bridge into the Cooum River. They told her the water would break her fall - they told her she'd emerge unscathed. But my childhood best friend, my ride or die - she landed on a rock. That incident led to them drifting apart.

I was devastated. I didn't leave my house for days. But I knew exactly how to get back at those reckless boys. I'd do exactly what they did to my friend.

Kalpana was willing to help me. I got her to start seeing Mahendran - they eventually got married, as you know. We both strategically moved to Basil Street then, so we could keep an eye on all 4 of our targets. Oh, those boys! Their fates were intertwined. They were destined to live together and die together - and they would have, if you girls hadn't meddled in our plans."

"I don't understand how you guys pulled off the actual thing. Both the murders were so hasty; they just seemed unplanned," commented Ananya.

"Can you let me finish? If I'm going to go out, I'd at least like the extent of my intelligence to be known.

I've been practising yoga for *years* now, to the point where I can contort myself into nearly inhumane poses. Watch this."

She twisted herself into the human equivalent of a *murukku*. Everybody inhaled in shock.

"Yes, see? It took a really long time, but I was able to train Kalpana to do the same. Now came the question of getting into their houses. Mahendran wouldn't be an issue. Kalpana and I came up with a plan, though. She convinced Mahendran to shut down his old business - a travel agency - and start

Organic Universe. That way, we could take advantage of its home delivery subscription. One of us would leave a package at the victim's gate, ring the doorbell, and hide outside their house. When they went to retrieve the package, we'd sneak in and use our contortion skills to hide inside an empty cabinet in their kitchen. It was a surefire way to stay safe - a bedroom cupboard would have been too risky.

Then came the actual murder. You see, with my limited knowledge of Ayurveda and Kalpana's knowledge of food science, we were able to put our heads together and come up with a potent medicine that triggers extreme hunger at very specific times. We snuck this into the groceries they ordered. That was how we lured them to the kitchen.

Killing Madhavan was really tricky. I didn't even do it - Kalpana did. I only killed Mahesh. Madhavan was apparently really good at self-defence - he put up a fight. Kalpana had to use the knife she had with her for emergencies and stab him. That was when our real plan came into play.

The 2 of us did extensive research to find a certain pulse point on the body that would cut off blood supply to the lungs if we pressed it hard enough for a whole minute. And so, after he was weakened by the knife, she took him out using that point.

That was exactly what I did to Mahesh. I hid in his fridge and *froze* until he got hungry. I did some minor damage to him with my knife and took him out."

The entire room stood there in shock, frozen, digesting every word that she had just said. Kalpana laughed at their gobsmacked expressions.

Shanaya broke the silence. "Why did both murders take place at 6:10, one day apart?"

"Darling, that's just Organic Universe's delivery subscription system!" Kalpana guffawed.

• • •

"Girls, I know I don't always appreciate your contributions to this city, but thank you. You saved 2 lives by piecing all that information together," admitted Vardarajulu.

"Detective, we still want closure," insisted Ananya. "What was in that envelope Sunita aunty gave you?"

"Was it a bribe?" asked Kyra.
"Or a love letter?" added Shanaya.

"Why did you clear the team out after receiving it?" Alana piped up.

"Wha- how did you even know about that? Girls, it was Madhavan's *will*," he huffed. "You guys suspected *me*?"

"Oh, oops."

"Well, to be fair, you've always acted really suspicious and cold around us," sighed Alana.

"This is really humiliating for me to admit as a professional detective and an adult man, but I was insecure," Vardarjulu revealed. "But it would be criminal - pun intended - if I didn't recognise your contributions to this city, girls. I'd really like it if we could work together on more cases in the future. I have my sources, and they told me just how much research you put in."

"I guess we really aren't shutting the agency down now, huh?" asked Alana.

Shanaya smiled and threw an arm across her shoulder. "Wasn't that obvious by Chapter 2?"

"Wait, what?" Kyra looked confused. "Chapter?"

Nevertheless, she and Ananya leaned in to hug the other 2.

They had made their mark, and peace had been restored to Basil Street again.